MURDER BEFALLS US

COZY MYSTERY TAILS OF ALASKA, BOOK 2

PATTI BENNING

SUMMER PRESCOTT BOOKS PUBLISHING

Angie Seaver dropped the two batter-covered fish fillets in the pan, listening to the satisfying sizzle for a moment before turning her attention to the batch of fries that was seconds away from being done. She watched the timer, waiting until it hit zero before she lifted the basket out of the oil and set it in the holder above the vat. The golden-brown wedges of potato looked perfect. She smiled to herself. She was getting better at this.

She heard Betty call another order out, and hurried over to the window to grab it. A chicken salad sandwich with fries and cottage cheese, a meal that sounded good enough to make her stomach growl. A glance at the clock told her she only had twenty minutes left on her shift. She would get lunch after, before heading home.

After flipping the fish fillets, she grabbed two slices of bread and slid them into the toaster, jiggling the lever just so to make sure it stayed down. After a few weeks, the little idiosyncrasies of the kitchen were almost like second nature to her. She was relearning everything she had forgotten in the years since she had last worked there, and then some.

She plated the fries, served a small amount of cottage cheese into a bowl, then turned her attention back to the fish, which was done. She slid the still sizzling fillets onto a plate which she had prepared a few minutes ago, then carried it over to the window.

"Table five," she called out. She didn't wait to see if Betty had heard her — Betty *always* heard her — before going back to finish the order with the chicken salad sandwich.

There wasn't another order to fill, so after handing the plate with the sandwich on it over to Betty, she began cleaning up. She had learned to tidy up fast during the times there was a lull, because if she didn't, the mess would pile up behind her as she worked.

She had just finished scrubbing the last pan when the door to the kitchen banged open. Expecting to see Betty, she was surprised when she looked up and saw her father. Then she glanced at the clock and realized her shift had ended. She was free to go.

"Busy day?" her father asked as he tied on his apron and walked over to the sink to scrub his hands. Angie left the water on for him and began drying her own hands on a clean towel.

"It wasn't that bad early in the morning," she said. "But it did get pretty busy for a while later on. Betty said there's some sort of game at the school tonight, and dinner will probably be crazy. Do you want me to come back and help out?"

He shook his head. "Grace is going to come in. Your mother mentioned she might like to come into town later today, though, if you're available."

"I'll definitely make time for that," she said. She pulled open the fridge and was eyeing the container of chicken salad when her father spoke again.

"A friend of yours is at table two. She caught me when I was coming in and I promised to send you out soon."

"A friend? Oh! Maggie." Angie shut the fridge in a hurry. "I completely forgot I promised her we could get lunch together."

"I saw a family of four getting out of their car in the parking lot. You'd better hurry if you want to get your orders in before they do."

"Thanks, Dad," she said. Over the past few weeks, they had gradually begun to pick up a rapport with each other. It was still strange, sometimes, to be back here after so long, but she was getting used to it.

She paused by the door to hang up her apron — which boasted a freshly printed name tag on the breast pocket — and then pushed through to the dining area. It was a sunny, clear day, and even though the kitchen was well lit, it was windowless. The bright sunlight coming in from the wide picture windows at the front of the restaurant made her feel like she had just stepped out of a cave.

"Hey, Angie!"

Maggie had spotted her before she'd even had a chance to look for her friend. Grinning, Angie headed toward the booth the other woman had claimed.

"I hope I didn't keep you waiting for long," she said, not wanting to mention that she had completely forgotten about their lunch plans. It wasn't a good excuse, but she *had* been busy the past few days.

"Nope, I got here just as your father was pulling in. It was perfect timing."

"That's good," Angie said. She eyed the group of four that was coming through the front door. "Do you know what you want? We should get our orders in soon, it looks like it's about to get busy."

"I always get the same thing," her friend said with a shrug. "The turkey club on rye. I've ordered it what, like three times while you were on shift?"

"It's hard to keep things straight when I'm in the kitchen," Angie admitted. "I just make the orders as fast as I can and call out table numbers."

"True." Her friend smiled at her. "Shall we order? I don't want to be in a rush, but I do have to pick up Josh in about an hour."

"Of course."

Angie met Betty's eyes and nodded. The older woman came over and took their orders, promising to bring the drinks out soon. It felt odd to be getting served at the diner. While she ate there a lot, it was usually back in the kitchen, after having put the food together herself. It would be nice to eat her dad's cooking for a change. He had always been a genius with food.

Betty came back within minutes with a coffee for Angie and a hot chocolate for Maggie. Once she was gone, a slightly awkward silence settled over their table. The two women had been close friends years ago, but both of them had gone separate directions with their lives and had fallen out of touch. Now they were getting to know each other all over again.

"Any luck with your brother?" Maggie asked at last.

"Oh, yeah. He actually bought the plane tickets. Emailed me a copy of the receipt and everything, since he knew I wouldn't believe him. I could practically hear the 'I told you so' through the computer screen."

Her friend giggled. "Did he actually say that?"

"No, but I know he was thinking it." Angie smirked. "The only way I could convince him to come and visit was by telling him I knew there was *no way* he would ever come back. He just had to prove me wrong."

"How long has it been since you've seen him?"

"Ten years," she said, shaking her head. "Same as with my parents. He moved out to Florida and pretty much cut off contact with everyone. I'd get friendly-enough replies to the emails I sent on holidays, but we didn't really start talking again until a couple of years ago when his fiancée — then girlfriend — found my profile on social media and sent me a friend request. She and I chatted for a while, and then eventually he started sending me messages too. We've kind of gotten back into an easy, teasing rela-tionship like we had before, but it's not quite as relaxed. There's still a lot neither of us will talk about with each other."

Her friend gave her a sad smile. "It can't be easy. Your family pretty much imploded after Katy's acci-dent. I wish I had been there more for you."

"There wasn't anything you could have done that you didn't do," Angie said firmly. "We were young, barely out of our teen years. You had — and have — your own life to worry about. I'm just glad that we're here now, talking to each other and getting to be friends again."

"Me, too. It's so nice to have someone I can just relax and have fun around. It's hard being a single mother, especially in such a small town. Everyone knows that Josh's father left me, and I feel like it's all anyone sees when they look at me."

"I know how this place can be." She grinned. "Don't worry, when I look at you, I still see the teenage version of you who helped me sneak out and go to that dance even though I was grounded. You know what, I think my mom probably still has some of my old yearbooks packed away somewhere. I should find the one from our senior year and show Josh what your hair looked like."

"My son would never let me live it down," Maggie groaned. The two of them laughed, and Angie sipped her coffee, feeling lighter than she ever thought she would after returning home.

2

As the date of her brother's visit approached, Angie found herself beginning to get nervous. Had she made a mistake in badgering her brother and his fiancée to come visit? Maybe it would have been better to start with something less demanding than a two week stay. If tensions got too high, the two of them could always get a motel in town, she supposed. She knew how happy her mother was that their guests would be staying at the house, and all Angie could do was cross her fingers and hope it went well. *It had better*, she grumbled to herself as she struggled to put the fitted sheet on the bed in the guest room. She had spent the weekend cleaning out the room, which had become a mix of storage room and failed exercise room. While her mother was good company, Angie had done all of the heavy lifting, and her body was definitely complaining.

At least everything was ready now. Her brother and his fiancée would be flying in in two days, and they would find a lovely guest bedroom waiting for them, along with some of her brother's favorite foods and a carbonated water drink that he had told them his fiancée just had to have. Even though she hadn't seen her brother in person for over a decade, his fiancée was the one she was most nervous about finally meeting. What would it be like to live with a complete stranger for two weeks?

A black bundle of fur came streaking into the room, tearing across the top of the bed and wrecking all of Angie's work with the fitted sheet before leaping off and turning on a dime to hide under the bed. Angie stumbled back, wincing. One of the cat's claws had caught her hand.

"What —" She cut her exclamation off when she heard barking from downstairs. With a sigh, she straightened the sheet then went downstairs, leaving the door to the guest room open so the cat — she hadn't had a chance to see if it was Chess or Checkers — could come out when it was ready.

In the living room, she found a husky barking from behind the collapsible pen he was in. He had a shaved patch on his hind leg, with a mostly healed injury partially visible. Next to the pen, another husky, this one red and white and significantly older, was lounging on the floor.

"Petunia, control your grandson," Angie said to the older dog. Turning to the dog in the pen, she waggled a finger in admonishment. "Oracle, you're supposed to be resting, not tormenting the cats."

The barking stopped when he heard his name, and Oracle put his paws up on top of the edge of the pen, looking at her eagerly. She relented and patted the top of his head.

"I guess you're probably just bored. But no more lying in wait for the cats and then jumping at them, okay? You'll be back out with the other dogs soon enough."

She pet the dog some more, feeling bad for him — though not quite as bad as she felt for the terrified cat under the bed upstairs. He was a young dog, and full of energy. He didn't know how to live in the house, and he didn't understand that it was just temporary while he recovered from his injury. All he knew was that he was bored, too hot, and that cats were fun to scare.

"Angie?" Her mother's quiet voice came from behind her. "Don't you have a date with Malcolm soon? I thought you'd be getting ready for it."

"It's not a date," she replied, turning away from the dogs. "But I do need to go get ready. One of the cats is hiding under the bed in the guest room, so don't shut the door. Oracle scared the poor thing again."

"I think your father plans to take him out to the dog yard tomorrow, if his vet appointment gives him the all clear." Her mother walked over to the dog and patted him, shaking her head. "I don't know who will be happier, Oracle or the cats. Go on and get ready for your date, dear. I don't want you to be late."

"Not a date," Angie muttered halfheartedly as she hurried down the hall to her room. She and Malcolm Miles had been spending a lot of time together over the past couple of weeks, but she didn't think they were dating. She wasn't actually sure. They went out to eat a lot, and he insisted on paying, but he hadn't so much as kissed her yet. It was possible he was taking things slow — he did have kids, so she could understand that — but more likely, he viewed her as a friend. Which she didn't mind. They definitely had enough in common to make great friends. But... she wanted to know for sure, because she definitely felt something for him other than simple friendship.

Tamping down the frustration, she got into the shower and scrubbed herself until her skin stung and her hair squeaked. The warm water was calming and helped to soothe the ache in her muscles from all of the heavy lifting she had done earlier in the day to help prepare for her brother's visit. By the time she had gotten out of the shower, dried her hair, and put a new outfit on, she was feeling much more optimistic. Date or not, she wanted to look her best for their outing. They were actually going out of town for dinner tonight, to a steakhouse halfway down the main road to the larger city. She knew that even if she didn't get any of her questions about their relationship resolved, it would be a fun evening. It always was.

3

Gillian and Joe's Steakhouse was in a long building in what felt like the middle of nowhere. If she hadn't already been familiar with the place, Angie might have wondered how on earth it managed to stay in business. There were maybe three houses in a five-mile radius of it, and it was a good forty-five minutes away from Lost Bay.

However, it was nearly the exact same distance from the larger city down the coast, and it was one of the nicest restaurants in the area. While it wasn't conveniently located for anyone, it was still well located, since anyone driving down to the city was bound to pass it, and with almost no competition, it was *the* place to stop at on the long drive to civilization. Plus, they served really good food.

Angie's family had gone there every Sunday for as long as she could remember all the way through high school, though they had stopped after all of their children had moved out. She had known the original owners, a married couple who had named the restaurant after themselves, and had heard through the grapevine that their daughter had inherited it when they retired.

Stepping through the doors into the darkly lit main dining room was like stepping into her past. The same old shuffleboard table was sitting along the side wall, and the decor was mostly what she remembered, though by the look of it the booths had been reupholstered and the walls had been repainted at some point. The restaurant still had a smoking side and a nonsmoking side, which was strange to Angie after spending so much time in California, where smoking in restaurants was banned.

"Party of two?" the hostess asked.

They nodded their affirmative, and the young woman led her and Malcolm to a secluded booth at the far side of the restaurant. It was still early in the evening, and the place wasn't very busy. Angie was glad — that meant that with luck, their food would come out quickly. She was hungry.

"So, how was your weekend?" he asked her as they settled in.

"Busy," she admitted. "I've been helping my mother get the house tidied up for my brother and his fiancée. The whole nine yards — we even moved the fridge to clean under it. It made me realize just how much she and my father probably did when they were getting ready for me to come back and stay with them. They completely redid the bedroom and bathroom that I took over. I feel bad, like I should have appreciated it more."

"I'm sure they know you do appreciate it," he said. "The first few days after you moved back were... kind of crazy. I think everyone was a bit distracted."

"True. Hopefully my brother's visit won't be anywhere near as exciting. Anyway, how was your weekend?"

"Great." His face relaxed into a smile. "I spent most of my time with the kids. I've been showing them how to take care of the dogs. They love it all, of course. Sometimes I wonder if the dogs are the ones they really want to visit, and I just happen to be there."

Angie laughed. "It's good for them, learning how to take care of animals. I'm glad they like it."

"Did you like it, when you were growing up? I know your dad has had dogs pretty much his whole life."

"I did and I didn't," she admitted. "I loved the dogs themselves, of course, but waking up at five in the morning to go outside in the freezing cold to feed them and get them fresh water before school was miserable. My siblings and I all took turns doing it. We were all expected to help with chores. I went through phases where I hated it, of course, but overall I think it was great. How many kids grow up with a dog sled team? I didn't really realize how lucky I was until I moved out to California, actually."

"Do you miss it? California, I mean, not your childhood."

"I miss the warmth," she said. "Being in southern California is a little bit like always being on vacation. But... I don't regret moving back here. This is home. None of us expected my mother's illness to get as bad as it did as quickly as it did, and I know I would have always regretted it if I had stayed away. I know it probably seems silly, to move back home in your thirties and throw away a decently paying office job to work at a diner, but I'm happy I did it."

"I don't think it's silly," he said with a smile. "There's more to life than just making money and having a fancy sounding job. I wish I'd learned that a long time ago. But I'm happy where I am now, and I definitely don't regret the path I took, since if I'd done something differently, I wouldn't have had my kids."

"It always comes back to family, doesn't it?"

They traded smiles. Angie was about to speak again, to bring up a lighter topic for their conversation, when a man stopped in front of their table, his eyes glued to her face.

"Um, excuse me?" she said after a few seconds passed.

"Angie? Angie Seaver?"

"That's me." She forced herself not to sigh. Moments like this had happened all too often over the weeks since she had moved back. She had thought that she had gotten past most of it, but apparently not. She decided to take it as a compliment that she was still so easily recognized after ten years. She couldn't have aged *that* much, if people could tell who she was at a glance.

"It's Percy. Percy McDougal. I used to come over to your house all the time after school, remember?"

"Oh, yeah. Percy... wow, you've changed. I like the beard." She winced. That had probably been a weird thing to say, but she had been caught off guard and Malcolm was watching her with amusement in his eyes.

He stroked it, then grinned. "So, is your brother back too?"

"No, but he's coming to visit for a couple weeks. Do you still talk to him?"

Percy and her brother had been best friends all through school, and he had been a fixture at their house. She didn't know exactly what had happened to him after he graduated. He had left town, but had apparently come back at some point.

"We're friends on social media, but don't talk much," he said. "Man, I'm only visiting for a short time too. I live in Anchorage now, I just come back a couple times a year to say hi to the folks. We should throw a party, get all of the old crew back together. I heard Maggie O'Brien moved back too. It would be just like old times."

"That might be fun," she said. "I'd have to talk to my parents. I'm staying with them for the time being, and my brother and his fiancée will be staying there for their visit as well."

"*Just* like old times," he said with a laugh. "I'll send him a message and let him know I'm visiting as well. Maybe we can make up for never having a high school reunion. Here's my card. You should keep in touch too. It was nice to see you again."

She took the card he handed her, and raised her eyebrows when she saw the initials after his name. He was doing well. She had never imagined that he would go on to get a PhD.

"I'll keep it," she promised him. "It was nice to see you again as well."

"You too." He blinked, as if noticing Malcolm for the first time. "Uh, sorry if I intruded on your date. I'll leave you alone now. See you in a few days, hopefully!"

With that, he wandered off and Angie turned her

attention back to Malcolm. He seemed amused, not annoyed, by the interruption, which she was glad about.

"Does *everyone* in this town know you?" he asked. "I think someone has recognized you every single place we've gone together."

"Well... I did spend a lot of my time during the summers helping out at the diner," she said. "It's a popular restaurant, pretty much everyone in Lost Bay has been there at some point. Everyone knew the owner's kids."

He shook his head, chuckling. "It's a strange sort of celebrity, but it certainly makes for interesting dates."

Angie grinned. He had called their outings dates. It looked like she had her answer, and she hadn't even had to ask.

4

After getting home from the diner the next day, Angie quickly showered and changed into nicer clothes, then joined her parents in the kitchen where they were having a somewhat tense discussion on what to make for dinner that night.

"We're not having burgers, Rod," her mother snapped. "We haven't seen him for over ten years. He's finally coming back to visit, and you want to feed him something he could get at any diner or fast food restaurant."

"Anise, he's coming here to see us. He's not going to care if the food isn't fancy. Plus, he likes burgers."

"Actually..." Angie began, somewhat hesitantly. Her parents turned to her, both of them looking as if they

hadn't realized she was standing there. "He's a vegetarian now. He eats seafood still, I think, but
that's it."

They stared at her for a long moment, then her
father shook his head. "How come you know that
and we don't?"

"Because I talk with him online," she said. "I see the
articles he shares and the things his friends post. He
decided to start being a vegetarian a couple years
ago. His fiancée mostly is too, but she eats chicken
and he doesn't. Trust me, they'll both be happy with
salmon or something."

Her father sighed. "Fine, fish for dinner it is. I guess
I'll just feed the dogs the ground beef I brought
home from the restaurant, since it's going to go to
waste otherwise." He stomped out of the kitchen.
Angie could hear his footsteps all the way down the
hall. When she heard her parents' bedroom door
slam shut, she turned to her mother.

"What on earth is he so upset about?" she asked.

Her mother sighed. "He's just anxious about seeing
your brother again. You know how similar he and
Jason can be. They're both stubborn, and convinced

that they're always the one in the right. Your brother hasn't stayed in touch with us as much as you, and I think what you said about him being a vegetarian now makes your father think he doesn't know his son anymore."

"Was he this bad while you two were preparing for me to come?"

"Oh, not at all," her mother said. "But you've always had a different relationship with him. You — both of you girls — were always daddy's girls. He was just excited. He never worried that he'd find a stranger waiting for him at the airport."

"Do you think I should offer to go pick them up tonight? Maybe it's best if Dad waits here."

"No, I don't think so. An hour in the car together will do them good."

The next few hours were a blur as they all did their last-minute preparations for the visit. Angie and her mother went to the store to get food, and Angie's father spent some time cleaning out his truck, going so far as bringing it into the barn so he could plug in the vacuum cleaner and clean the upholstery. At last, it was time for him to leave for the long trip to the airport. He seemed grim, and all Angie could do was hope that he and her brother didn't get into an argument before they even got home.

She finished unpacking the bags in the kitchen and brought the pack of bath soaps and salts she had bought for her brother's fiancée — her soon to be sister-in-law — to the upstairs bathroom. She took one last look around, making sure everything was in place, then went downstairs to help her mother cook.

Soon, the kitchen was heavy with the scent of dinner. They had decided on dill salmon, quinoa with garlic and spring onions, and her mother's famous homemade dinner rolls. For dessert, they had picked up a frozen chocolate cream pie. Working side by side with her mother brought back memories of helping cook for holidays and family get-togethers when she was younger. It was peaceful, and she found her worries melting away as she stirred the creamy dill sauce. *The kitchen really is the heart of the house*, she thought.

"It's been a long time since I've made these," her mother said as she covered the dough for the rolls with a hand towel. "I hope I remembered everything."

"They'll be perfect," Angie said. "You should have opened a bakery. Your rolls are amazing."

"It's my greatest gift in the kitchen. You and your father inherited the cooking gene. Besides, the rolls are a labor of love. Some of the magic would be lost if I made hundreds every day for strangers."

She could understand that. While she enjoyed cooking at the diner and always put her best foot forward with each plate she made, there was something about cooking for family that she just couldn't put her finger on. It made all the difference, though. She didn't think she was ever this relaxed at the diner.

"We'll wait to put the salmon in until Dad calls to tell us they're almost home," she decided. "We don't want the fish to get cold. Everything else can be kept warm on the stovetop."

"It shouldn't be too long," Angie said, glancing at the clock. "I can't believe he's actually coming to visit."

"Me either." Her mother smiled. "I'm glad he is

though. I'm happy I get to meet his fiancée. Do you know much about her?"

"Not too much. She seems nice. I think she is the one who encouraged him to come back and make amends." She hesitated. "I don't know if it's my place to say this, but she mentioned to me in an email that she wants all of us at their wedding. I know her family is really close, so it's probably important to her that his family is involved too."

"Well, I guess I should direct my thanks to her." The older woman sank down into a chair at the kitchen table. "Thanks for all of your help these past few days, Angie. I couldn't have done it without you."

"That's what I'm here for," she said. "I'm happy to help however I can. You and Dad have been trying to do things on your own for too long."

"I know it's hard for him to take care of me and also run the diner. He hasn't complained, but I can tell having you here has taken a load off."

"Good. You two should have told me you were having troubles earlier. I would have come."

"Well, you're here now. That's what matters."

They smiled at each other. Before either of them could say anything else, the phone rang. Angie picked it up.

"It's Dad," she told her mother after a moment, putting her hand over the receiver. "They'll be here soon. They're just past the diner right now."

Her mother nodded and got up to see if the rolls had raised enough. Angie finished the conversation with her father, said her goodbyes, and ended the call. She put the salmon in the oven, feeling a twist of nerves in her stomach. For the first time in ten years her family would be together again — most of them, anyway. This visit would set the tone for the rest of their lives.

5

The front door opened, letting in a blast of cold air and the sounds of conversation. Angie hurriedly rinsed off the last pot and put it in the drying rack before drying her hands and helping her mother up and out of her seat.

"Here, take my arm," she said. "I'll help you over to the door."

"Thanks," the older woman said. "The walker would just get in the way. Goodness knows how much luggage they brought."

The two of them walked slowly out of the kitchen and down the hall. Angie tried not to feel impatient, but she was bursting with eagerness to see her brother and meet his fiancée. At last they came to the front entrance way, where three people were busy taking off their warm outerwear.

"Angie! Mom!"

She barely had time to brace them both before a pair of strong arms wrapped around her for a long second. A moment later they vanished as her brother turned to hug their mother. He stepped back, grinning.

"Jason," their mother said. "Goodness. Look at you. It's been so long." She wavered on her feet, and Angie reached out to support her.

"I know. I'm sorry about that. How are you doing?"

"Not so bad, lately. Now, why don't you introduce us to your lovely fiancée?"

"Oh, yeah! Mom, Angie, this is Lydia. Lydia, this is my mom and Angie."

A pretty woman with bobbed blonde hair and an easy smile stepped forward. "It's so nice to meet you both. Thank you for inviting me to stay with you."

"Of course," their mother said. "You can call me Anise. How was your drive from the airport?"

"Long," Lydia said, laughing. "When Jason told me you guys live in the middle of nowhere, he wasn't joking. It's beautiful here, though. Very different from Florida."

An insistent beep started to sound from the kitchen. "That's the salmon," Angie said. "You should all go sit down. I'll get the food."

It wasn't long before they were all seated at the table, serving dishes full of steaming food in the center. Angie's mother kept smiling at Jason and Lydia. Her father hadn't said much, and she was curious to find out if he had actually spoken at all during the long drive back from the airport, or if they had just sat in silence the entire time.

"This looks lovely," Lydia said.

"Angie's the one who told us about your dietary preferences," her father said gruffly. "You have her to thank. It does look good, though. You two did a good job."

"Are these your famous rolls?" Jason asked, grabbing two out of the basket. "Man, it's been a long time since I've had these. Here, Lydia, try one."

The conversation stayed on food for the rest of the

meal. Angie was glad that the meal had turned out so well, though her father still seemed slightly annoyed about the burgers. He didn't talk much while they ate, but seemed somewhat mollified when Lydia told him how much Jason talked about the family diner and the food they served there.

"He always compares other diners to yours when we go out to eat," she said. "Before we decided to change our diets, he would make me the best burgers ever, and said he learned how from you."

Angie smiled at that. Lydia was a skilled conversationalist and always seemed to know what to say when awkward silences fell. Talking with someone through emails wasn't the same as meeting them face to face, and she had been prepared for things to be awkward between the two of them, but instead she found herself quite liking the other woman.

At last came the time for them to clear the table and bring out dessert. Jason jumped up to help Angie, telling everyone else to stay seated. They each grabbed a couple plates and carried them into the kitchen. Angie pulled open a drawer and started counting out dessert forks, when Jason put his hand on her shoulder.

"Thanks for convincing me to come back," he said. "I should have done it a long time ago."

"Then why didn't you?" she asked. Her tone was neutral and curious, but he still winced as if she had spoken to him in anger.

"Because I didn't know what to say to them," he finally admitted. "Do you know why I left in the first place?"

She shrugged. "I always assumed it was for the same reason that I did. Things were spiraling here, and everywhere I looked there were reminders of Katy. I felt like there was no future, like if I stayed here I would always be defined by what I had lost. I needed a fresh start, not so I could forget but so I didn't have other people constantly remembering for me."

He tilted his head. "Well, I suppose it was partially for those reasons. Everywhere I looked, there were reminders and guilt. But that wasn't what made me decide to leave in the end. It was Dad."

"Dad? Why?"

"I bought the cell phone for her, you know," he said. "Katy wanted one for her graduation present. I bought it for her and was paying for her plan. Dad told me it was my fault that she died. That if I hadn't bought the phone for her, she'd still be here."

"Jason, that's horrible! He had no right to do that."

"It was right after the funeral. None of us were really thinking straight. But I just couldn't stay after that. It took me a long time to get over what he said, and by the time I started to think that maybe I should reach out, it had been too long and I didn't know where to start. Plus, Mom never knew and by then she had been diagnosed with Parkinson's and I didn't want to bring up old history during all of that. So I ended up just keeping my distance."

"Why are you telling me this now?"

"Because I want your advice." He sighed. "I don't know if I should bring it up with him, or wait for him to say something, or just pretend it never happened and enjoy the time here with you and Mom."

"I think if you want him to apologize, you're going to have to bring it up yourself," she said. "You know how Dad it."

"You're probably right. I'll give him a couple of days, at least. Everyone's having such a good time now, and I don't want to wreck it." He grinned at her. "Maybe after the party."

"You talked to Percy?"

"Yep. And I talked to Dad in the car. We're going to get people together this weekend. Dad's making burgers, and Mom's bringing out the old yearbooks. Percy said he'd call up some old friends. If there's anyone you want to invite, feel free. It will be nice to see everyone again."

"I'll see if Maggie can come," she said. "And..."

"And?"

"This guy I'm seeing, Malcolm. I might see if he wants to come too."

Her brother's grin widened, and he nudged her shoulder. "You didn't tell me you had a boyfriend. My little sister is growing up."

"Oh, shut up." She shoved him back. "He's not my boyfriend, we've just gone on a few dates so far. And aren't we a bit old for this sort of teasing?"

He ruffled her hair. "Never. You'll always be my little sister."

6

The next couple of days were more fun than Angie had dared hope for. Even though she spent a lot of time at the diner, she still managed to see a lot of her brother and his fiancée. They stopped in at least once every day, much to the delight of Betty, who considered herself something of a stand-in grand-mother. Angie knew that Jason was spending his days showing Lydia around town, going around to all of the places where he had made his childhood memories. She was sad to learn that she had missed him taking her out on one of her father's dog sleds with a small six dog team, but she couldn't help but grin as Lydia described how exhilarating it had been.

Saturday rolled around, and Angie was glad to be

able to sleep in a little bit. Working the morning shifts at the diner during the week meant that she woke up hours before the sun rose five days a week. It could get disheartening.

There wasn't much she had to do to prepare for the party. While she was busy working the day before, Jason and Lydia had gone shopping, buying all the food they could possibly need. When she stumbled out of bed shortly past eight, she was surprised to find Lydia vacuuming the living room while her mother folded laundry on the couch.

"Good morning," Lydia said brightly as she shut the machine off.

"Good morning." Angie fought back a yawn. "I can do that, you don't have to. I was going to do the cleaning this morning."

"I don't mind at all," Lydia said. "I know Jason kind of dragged you guys into this party. I'd feel bad if you had to do extra work because of it. I know how much work you do during the week."

"It was Percy's idea," Angie said. "But it should be fun."

"Who's Percy?"

"Oh, he was Jason's best friend when they were younger. He used to drag him into all kinds of stuff." She chuckled. "My dad used to say that Jason would follow Percy off a cliff. He was always the instigator when they got into trouble. I guess he must be sort of a natural leader — it sure paid off. He gave me his business card the other day and I looked him up. He's leading a team of marine biologists in Anchorage."

"Wow. Jason always tells me that was his dream job. I bet he's jealous."

Angie laughed. "Probably. Anyway, if you're sure you want to vacuum, I'm going to go take a shower and get ready for the day. I'll help set everything up after."

"Go ahead." Lydia waved her away. "I've got this. I've already gotten halfway down my checklist, see?"

Angie looked to where the other woman gestured, to see a small notebook lying open on the coffee table, a list of chores written in neat lines on the page. She chuckled. "You're more organized than I am. I'll leave you to it."

People began arriving shortly after two in the afternoon. Malcolm was the first to get there, bearing a gift of wine that he told her he had been saving for a special occasion.

"I can't think of a better occasion than your brother's welcome home party," he said. "Wait, why didn't you get a party?"

Angie wrinkled her nose. "Because I like living my life a bit on the quieter side. I was *hoping* to move back here without making a big deal about it, but the town didn't let that happen. I'm glad we're doing this, though. It really will be nice to get everyone together again."

"Are you sure I'm welcome?" he asked. "I mean, I didn't grow up here."

"Of course you are. It will be a great chance for you to meet more people. Come on, we've got appetizers. Lydia made crab rangoons that are to die for."

A few hours later, the house was full of laughter and noise. Her father was in the kitchen making burgers on a stove top grill and chatting with one of the neighbors, who had caught word of the gathering and invited himself over. Her brother was in his element, going around the house and catching up with everyone he hadn't seen in years. Lydia followed along with him, looking tolerant and slightly amused. Angie wasn't surprised when he dragged yet another old friend over to her and asked her if she remembered who he was.

"Um, Oliver, right?"

The man nodded. "Yep. It's nice to see you again, Angie. I heard you were back."

"Who hasn't?" She grinned at him. "So, what are you doing these days?"

"Teaching in the computer lab at the school," he said. "It's not glamorous, but it pays the bills."

"I never thought you'd be a teacher," her brother said, shaking his head.

"I never thought you'd move to Florida," Oliver retorted. "Life never goes according to plan."

"Well, for some of us it does."

Angie turned to see where her brother was looking and saw Percy walking toward them with a woman on his arm. He spotted her looking and waved.

"There you guys are. Sorry we're late, we got held up.

I'd like to introduce my wife, Esme. This is Jason, his sister Angie, and one of our old friends, Oliver."

"Nice to meet you all," the woman said. "I've heard stories about the trouble your group got into as kids. When Percy told me you were having a get together, I just knew I had to come."

"It's nice to meet you too," Angie said. "Did you come all the way from Anchorage?"

Esme nodded. "I usually hold down the fort at home while Percy visits his parents here. It's hard for both of us to get time off work at the same time, but finally being able to meet all of his old friends was a chance I couldn't pass up."

"Pardon me," Percy said, interrupting politely. "Could I talk to you, Jason? It won't take long."

Angie saw her brother raise an eyebrow. "All right," he said. "If anyone comes looking for me, tell them I'll be down in a bit."

"I will," she promised. He and Lydia followed Percy away. She turned back to Esme. "Can I get you a drink? The refreshments are over here..."

The party continued, with Angie playing hostess in

her brother's absence. Things began to wind down, and she joined Malcolm on the couch in the living room.

"Hey," she said. "How are you doing?"

"I'm enjoying myself," he said. "How are you?"

"Exhausted," she said. "My brother vanished. I have no idea where he's gotten to. He should be playing host, not me. I think people are starting to leave, though. Have you seen Maggie?"

"You just missed her. She left about two minutes ago. She couldn't find you, so she asked me to tell you goodbye and that she had a good time, but that her son's babysitter can't stay too late tonight."

"That's too bad. I'm glad she enjoyed herself though. Do you want to —"

A sharp scream cut through her words. It sounded like it had come from outside. Conversation in the room died down as people looked toward the front window. Angie stood up, frowning. It was a cold night; she didn't know why anyone would be outside unless they were going directly to their car. Her heart stuttered as she realized who the scream was likely from — Maggie.

She hurried toward the front door, Malcolm following her. She was in the middle of pulling on her boots when the door slammed open and her friend practically fell inside. Her eyes were wide and panicked, and Angie put her hands on the other woman's shoulders to help calm her down. Her first thought was that a bear or a moose might have wandered into the yard, but no, she would hear the dogs barking if that was the case.

"Mags, what's going on?" she said.

"Th-there's a body," her friend stammered. "Outside, in the snow."

7

For the first time since people had begun to arrive at the party, complete silence fell over the house. Angie stared at her friend in shock, then released her shoulders and pulled her boots the rest of the way on, grabbing her coat from the closet and shrugging it on as she stepped out onto the porch. Malcolm was right behind her, and she heard the sounds of other people getting their own shoes and coats on as well.

"Where —"

"Over here," Maggie said, interrupting her before she could even finish her question. Angie followed her friend around the side of the house. She saw the person lying in the snow the second she rounded the corner. He or she would have been easily visible from where Maggie's car was parked.

He, she thought. She recognized Percy almost immediately, and from the angle at which his neck was, there was no question that he was dead.

Malcolm put a hand on her shoulder to steady himself, and she realized she had come to a dead stop mid-step. Her eyes were glued to the body as her brain tried to catch up with reality.

"I... I don't understand," she said. "I just saw him... he was fine."

"The balcony," Malcolm said. She looked up, and understood immediately what he meant. There was a small balcony on the upper level of the house, where her mother used to take her tea in the mornings. Percy was lying beneath it. *He must have fallen*, she thought.

Before she could even begin to wonder how he had fallen two stories to his death, her father made it out of the house, followed by a couple of guests. They all stopped and stared in shocked silence at the body, until her father spoke.

"Everyone, go back inside. Angie, call the police."

She hesitated, looking back at Percy one last time before following Malcolm to the front door. She pushed her way inside, ignoring the questions that pelted her as she rushed toward the kitchen, where the land line was. She picked it up and dialed the emergency number, stumbling through her words when the dispatcher answered.

She was asked to wait on the line after telling the woman what had happened. While she stood there silently with the phone pressed between her cheek and shoulder, her hands nervously wringing themselves in front of her, her brother stepped into the kitchen.

"Hey, Ange. What's happening?" he asked.

She just stared at him, unable to form the words to tell him that his friend was dead.

"Okay, we have an ambulance and patrol cars en route," the dispatcher said in her ear.

"Thank you," she said.

"Why's everyone standing in the living room?" her brother asked.

She covered the lower portion of the phone with her hand. "Go talk to Dad, Jason."

He frowned at her, but left the kitchen. She closed her eyes tightly, wishing frantically that this was all just a dream.

Her father didn't let any of the guests leave before the police arrived. The entire group waited silently indoors. Jason was standing angrily in a corner, while Lydia tried to comfort him. Angie and Malcolm stood quietly next to her father and Maggie, who was trying not to cry. Sitting on the couch was Esme, Percy's wife, sobbing quietly into Angie's mother's arms.

Malcolm was watching out the window, and was the first to see the emergency vehicles when they arrived. "They're here," he said softly.

Angie looked at Maggie. "Mags, they're going to want to talk to you. They're probably going to want to talk to all of us, but especially you since you found him. Are you up to it?"

She nodded, taking a deep breath and pushing her shoulders back. "I am."

"Looks like your father's here," Angie added,

glancing out the window herself. Her own father, who had kept his boots and coat on, had already slipped out the front door to greet the police.

"He is? I guess I shouldn't be surprised. That makes me feel a little better, at least."

Maggie's father was Detective O'Brien, and he handled most of the serious crimes in Lost Bay. He took his job seriously, but had a soft spot for his daughter.

"Let's get our stuff back on, Mags. Dad shouldn't have to handle all of this on his own."

Her friend nodded. Angie felt her heart twist at the look on the other woman's tear-streaked face. She had always been the more timid of the two of them, and had never handled emotional situations well. She knew how hard this must be for her friend.

Detective O'Brien spotted them when they walked outside. Angie saw him do a doubletake when he saw his daughter. He hurried over, waving away the officer who was talking to him.

"Mags?" he said. "What are you doing here?"

"I was invited to the party," she said. "And... I'm the one who found the body."

He frowned and glanced at Angie. She felt sixteen again, as if she was the one responsible for getting them into trouble.

"Officer Jace will take care of the body and the documenting of the scene. I want you both to tell me exactly what happened."

"I was about to go home," Maggie said. "I was just scraping the snow off of my car when I saw what looked like someone lying in the snow by the side of the house. I was a little bit worried, but I didn't think it was anything serious. I guess I just thought it was someone being silly or something. I... I walked over to see if they were okay, but they didn't answer when I called out, and when I got closer, I saw the way he was lying..." She trailed off with a shudder. "Then I ran back inside and told Angie what I saw and she and Malcolm and her father came out and then her father told Angie to go inside and call the police. And that's it. I didn't even realize it was Percy until Angie said something."

"So you knew the deceased?"

Maggie nodded. "I went to school with Percy. He was best friends with Angie's brother. You've probably met him."

Detective O'Brien sighed and rubbed at his temples. "Probably. Who all was at the house tonight?"

Maggie turned to Angie, who answered. "... plus a few significant others who I don't know that well because they're not from town or they're not close to my age," she said when she was done. "Everyone's still here except for a few people who left early. My dad thought you might want to talk to them."

"Good thinking on his part. That sounds like quite the party," he said. "Any special occasion?"

"My brother's welcome home party," she said.

"Ah, I'd heard he was visiting. Was there alcohol at this party?"

"We had some beer and wine, but nothing very strong. People can't exactly take taxi's home."

"Do you remember if the deceased had much to drink?"

"I don't think so, but I wasn't paying particular attention to him," she said. She knew what he was think-

PATTI BENNING

ing. Percy would have to be pretty unsteady on his feet to fall from the balcony accidentally.

"Did he get into any significant arguments tonight, or do you know of any other reason why someone might wish him harm?"

"No to both questions. Everyone seemed to be in a good mood."

"Thanks. I think that's all I need from you two for now. Are you okay to drive home, Maggie, or do you want me to give you a ride to your apartment when I'm done?"

"I'll be okay," she said. "I have to pick up Josh, and I'm already late."

She and Angie said a quick goodbye, with a promise to talk more tomorrow. Angie watched as her friend got into her car and drove away, then went inside where the detective was questioning the other guests. She did not look around the side of the house where the police and paramedics were examining the body.

8

Angie knew that the shock of Percy's death would echo through the town for weeks. The mystery surrounding his death would make it even worse. How had he fallen from the balcony? That question plagued her all through the night. She slept fitfully, grateful for Petunia's comforting warmth at the foot of the bed whenever she woke up.

She finally gave up on sleep when the glowing numbers of the clock on her nightstand told her it was seven in the morning. She still felt exhausted, but lying in bed wasn't helping anything. Keeping quiet, so as not to wake anyone else, she tiptoed through the house to the front door, where she let Petunia outside to take care of her morning business. Oracle had been moved back to the dog yard the night before, and the house felt strangely calm without his rambunctious energy.

Once Petunia came back inside, Angie made her way to the kitchen. The warm light coming from the room told her that someone else was already up. She was unsurprised to find her brother sitting at the kitchen table, turning a coffee cup slowly around in his hands.

"Hey," she said softly.

He looked up. "Hey. You're up early."

"So are you. I couldn't sleep."

He nodded and turned his attention back to his drink. "There's more coffee in the pot. I just made it."

"Thanks."

She gave Petunia a scoop of dog food in her bowl, then grabbed herself a mug from the cupboard and spent a few minutes preparing her drink. She didn't say anything as she sat down across from her brother. They sat together for a while, sipping their coffee in silence other than for the crunching of kibble as the husky ate her breakfast.

"I think I was the last person to see him alive," her brother admitted after a while.

"Really?"

He nodded. "We talked on the balcony. The rest of the house was too crowded. He offered me a job. We chatted for a bit, then I went in and left him out there alone. That was the last time I saw him."

"I'm sorry." She hesitated. "Was that why he wanted to talk to you? The job offer?"

"Yeah. He was offering me a position at the center he works for. I would have been in charge of gathering and interpreting local weather data to track how temperature and precipitation levels affect the migratory habits of native species. He was so happy. I just can't believe that he's gone now."

"Do you think he slipped?"

Jason frowned. "I... don't know. There was some snow on the balcony, but it wasn't too bad. He hadn't been drinking much or anything. I don't see how he could have fallen over the railing."

"I'll have to ask Maggie, but I got the feeling her father wasn't convinced it was an accident." Detective O'Brien had spent hours at their house the night before, talking to each of the guests before they left for home, and then examining the balcony with painstaking thoroughness.

He scoffed. "It's a bit paranoid to think that someone murdered him, isn't it? I mean, come on, Angie, this is a small town. That sort of thing doesn't happen here."

"Didn't you read my email about what happened the first week I got here?" she asked.

"Well, yeah…" He looked away from her gaze. "Okay, so maybe it does happen. But that doesn't mean that murder is the answer to everything. Some things are just accidents."

"I wish I could believe that what happened to Percy was an accident," she said.

"You'd rather believe one of his friends killed him?"

"It's not about what I'd rather believe. It's about what I do believe," she bit back. "Obviously I have no idea what happened, but you've got to admit that it's at least a little bit suspicious. If Detective O'Brien is acting like it might not be an accident, then I'm going to go with that. If someone did kill him, they could be dangerous to other people too. I know you don't live here, but I do. It scares me to know that one of the people in this town, someone I might serve a burger to tomorrow, could be responsible for Percy's death."

He sighed. "You're right. I'm sorry. I just hate feeling like this. I keep wondering if there was something I could have done differently. If I had done the right thing, he might still be alive right now."

"Don't think like that," she said softly. "You couldn't have known what was going to happen."

"This whole thing is my fault. If I hadn't come back, there wouldn't have been a party, and he'd be fine right now."

"Jason. Stop it. It's *not* your fault. He's the one who wanted to have a party in the first place, remember? He wanted everyone to get together again. You were just planning on staying for a couple of weeks and visiting with us. The party wasn't your idea, and even if it was, that still wouldn't make what happened to him your fault. Come on, sitting here staring at an empty coffee cup isn't going to help matters. Help me clean up."

She watched with concern as her brother got up mutely, deposited his mug in the sink, then turned to her as if waiting for directions. This wasn't the Jason she knew. She could understand what he was going through, but it couldn't be healthy. *Maybe I can get Lydia to help him see that he's not responsible for what happened*, she thought as she put her own mug in the sink. *Otherwise he'll just go on blaming himself forever.*

"Do you want to pick up the trash while I do the dishes?" she asked. None of them had felt like cleaning up after the police left, so the house was still a mess.

He nodded and walked toward the door, pausing at the threshold and looking back at her. "Thanks, Ange. I know you're trying to help."

"Of course. That's what siblings do."

9

After a long day of cleaning, Angie collapsed into bed and fell asleep almost instantly. When she woke up to the beeping of her alarm the next morning, it took her a moment to remember why there was a heavy feeling of grief making her stomach twist.

Waking up early for the morning shift at the diner left no time for her to ruminate on what had happened over the weekend, but flashes of memory invaded her mind anyway. She was distracted enough that she barely made it to the restaurant in time to open, and could already tell that it wasn't going to be a good day. Distractions never bode well when she was in the kitchen.

The easy routine of opening helped her to organize her thoughts a bit, and she began to mentally go through the list of people who had attended the party while she worked. She had still been too shell shocked to really think clearly about it the day before, but now, with some distance from the incident, she felt her curiosity beginning to stir.

As she considered each and every person as a potential murderer, she felt her suspicions that Percy's death had been anything but an accident beginning to fade. She didn't know everyone who had attended, but she did know most of the same people Percy did, and for the life of her, she just couldn't fathom a motive. He didn't even live in Lost Bay anymore, for goodness sakes. It wasn't as if he was having an affair with someone's wife. Maybe she had been getting ahead of herself when she had talked to Jason on Sunday morning.

Still, try as she might, she couldn't figure out how he could accidentally fall from a balcony. It seemed like he would have had to be trying to do it to even come close, and a man who had just offered a childhood friend a job and who had brought his wife all the way from Anchorage to a welcome home party didn't seem like the sort of person who was considering ending it all.

"I know, I know. I should just let the police figure it out," she told the coffee machine as it gurgled at her. "But I can't help that I'm thinking about it. It's *weird.*"

The door to the kitchen opened and she jumped, looking up to see Theo walk in. He was in the process of peeling off his down coat, and was giving her an odd look.

"What?" she asked, looking down at her apron. She hadn't even started making food yet. Surely she hadn't managed to spill something on herself.

"I just thought I heard you talking to someone, that's all."

"I was just talking to myself, don't mind me," she said. "You're here early."

"Your dad asked me to stop in and do inventory," he said. "He usually does it, but he said something about it being a busy weekend and that he wouldn't have time this week."

"Oh, okay. Let me know if you need any help."

She considered asking if she could watch and maybe take notes, but decided against it. If her father wanted her to learn how to do inventory and make orders, he'd tell her. She wasn't sure exactly what her position really entailed here. He had told her that he needed her to act as manager when he couldn't be there, but in reality, she was more of a glorified fry cook. She didn't mind, not exactly, but she knew there was more to running the diner than learning how to cook food. Betty was getting close to retiring, and once she left, Angie had a feeling her father was going to be the only person who actually knew how to do everything that the diner needed to have done in order to run smoothly. She just wished he would let her do more.

She let Theo choose the radio station and they spent the morning working in companionable silence. There was a bit of a rush when the diner first opened, and she spent the first few hours running around in an effort to keep everyone's coffee mugs full and get their orders out on time. Relief came shortly before noon when Grace arrived. Angie smiled at the younger woman on her way through the dining area with a plate stacked high with pancakes. Grace smiled back, then raised her eyebrows in a silent question that Angie couldn't understand.

She got her answer when she returned to the

kitchen. "I was wondering how you're doing," Grace said. "I heard what happened at your house. I'm so sorry, that must have been terrible."

"How did you hear?" Angie asked, surprised that the news had gotten out already.

"Oh, it was in the paper on Sunday morning." Grace walked over to the nook where the employees kept their personal items and came back with a newspaper in her hand. "Betty brings this in every Sunday."

Angie looked at the paper and sighed. The headline read, *Town Local Found Dead After Party*. Lost Bay was a small town with an even smaller paper. She shouldn't have been surprised to find that they had jumped at the chance to print such an exciting story, even if it meant making last minute changes to the paper the night before it went out.

"Someone at the party must have contacted them," she said, skimming through the article. "This is horrible."

"Did they get something wrong?" Grace asked, taking the paper back and reading through it again.

"No, not really, though Percy wasn't really local

anymore, he was just back for a visit. I'm just imagining what his parents must have felt when they saw this on Sunday morning. It would be terrible to see. They would have only learned about his death a few hours before."

Grace blanched. "Oh, my goodness, I didn't even think about that. You're right, that is horrible." She folded the paper and put it back. "Do you know if they have any idea who killed him?"

"As far as I know, the police haven't yet determined whether it was homicide or an accidental death," Angie said. "I really don't know anything more than anyone else."

"Right. And you probably don't want to talk about it either. Sorry."

"It's okay." Angie gave her a tired smile. "I've been here all morning. Do you mind if I take a break from the kitchen for a while and bus tables? We can switch out again before my shift ends."

"Sounds good to me," Grace said cheerfully.

Angie liked busing tables and waiting. The dining area had large windows and always felt more cheerful than the kitchen. The gentle hum of conversation, punctuated by the occasional laugh or shriek of an upset child, made her feel like a part of something alive. It was nice to see people enjoying their food, to know that her family's restaurant was playing a part, no matter how small, in making people's days happier.

She spent some time walking around the room, stopping to refill coffee cups and sodas, and occasionally pausing to chat with someone she knew. It was a busy time of the year for them. They were near the path of the Iditarod dog race, which would be starting soon, and people from all over the country were coming to the state. Out-of-towners were always easy to identify, and she was always happy to stop and answer their questions. She knew that life in a small town in Alaska wasn't what most people were used to, and she enjoyed sharing some of her experiences with them.

It took her a while to make the rounds to all of the tables, and she didn't even notice who sat at the last one until she approached him.

"Oliver?"

He looked up and smiled when he saw her. "Hey, Angie. I thought I might see you here."

"I'm here pretty much every morning during the week," she said. "I thought you taught at the local school. Don't you have classes now?"

"I called in sick," he said. "Percy's death really shook me, and I know the students will all be talking about it today. This sort of stuff doesn't happen often in Lost Bay."

"Yeah. My brother's pretty upset about it too. I am as well, of course, but you guys knew him better."

"I think I stayed in touch with him more than your brother did," he said. "I had actually been emailing back and forth with him for about a month about a job opening at the research center he worked at. It just feels weird to know he's gone now, you know?"

"I do," she said. She hesitated. "What do you think happened? On the balcony, I mean."

"You mean, do I think it was an accident?"

She nodded.

"I think someone pushed him off," he said with a frankness that startled her. "I mean, come on. People don't just spontaneously fall over a railing. Even if he had slipped or something, he would have had time to grab at the edge and get his feet under him. To fall head first like that... someone had to have taken him by surprise."

"Do you... have any idea who might have done it?"

He shrugged. "I know he and his wife were having problems. I told the police as much. I guess there's nothing else I can do, so I've been trying not to dwell on it so much."

"Right." She frowned. "Thanks, Oliver. Sorry for asking you all that. You probably just want to eat in peace. Let me know if you need any refills, okay?"

"I will. Thanks, Angie."

10

"Coffee is the best part of life," Maggie moaned, sipping at the foam that was threatening to overflow from the paper cup.

Angie slid into the seat opposite her friend, her own cup of coffee in hand. The latte at Snow Grounds was a hundred times better than the black coffee they served at the diner, and she wasn't ashamed to admit it.

"I'm not going to argue against that," she said as she took a sip of her own foamy concoction. "I don't know how people made it through the day before coffee."

"Thanks for picking me up. Sorry for calling you while you were at work."

PATTI BENNING

"I don't mind at all. My shift was just about over, and Theo had already finished inventory and was ready to start his usual shift. Grace was there as well, and three of us working during lunch is overkill. Plus, you saved me from having to bring Oliver his fifth soda refill. He's been hiding out there for a couple of hours, and it was starting to get awkward."

She had been planning on going home after her shift at the diner and spending some time with her family, but when Maggie called her begging for help after getting a flat tire, she hadn't hesitated before agreeing to pick her up from the auto shop. Their rekindled friendship meant a lot to her, and if being a good friend meant getting a latte while they waited for the shop to get around to changing her tire, well, she wasn't complaining.

"I don't really remember him that well," Maggie admitted. "I know he was part of your brother's group of friends at school, but that's it. Why is he hiding in your diner?"

Angie explained about him calling in sick to work. "I don't know why he doesn't just go home, but I wasn't about to kick him out either. I know Percy's death

72

was hard on my brother. I can't imagine it's much easier for him."

"I'm upset enough about it, and I didn't even know Percy that well," her friend said with a sigh. "Joshua asked me why I was so sad when I picked him up Saturday night, and I didn't know what to say. Telling him that I found a dead body just seems like it would be too much for him, you know?"

"What did you end up telling him?"

"That a friend of mine passed away and even though I didn't know him very well, it was sad."

"That makes sense. You've got to think fast when you have kids, I guess. I don't think I have the knack for it. Malcolm's kids run circles around me."

Maggie gave her a small smile. "So you've been spending a lot of time with them? He must really like you."

"Nothing like that," Angie said. "He just brings them into the diner every weekend. They like the waffles there. We aren't anywhere near serious enough for him to actually introduce me to them as anyone other than 'Dad's friend who makes breakfast at the diner.'"

"Still, that's really sweet of him. I wish — hey, isn't that your brother?"

Angie followed her friend's gaze. Sure enough, her brother and Lydia were walking up to the cafe. She half got out of her seat to wave at them. They waved back, and a moment later, they joined the two women at their table.

"Fancy seeing you here," Angie said, grinning. Despite everything that had happened, she was still so *happy* to have her family reunited.

"We were going to surprise you at the diner, but you had already left," Jason said. "I guess deciding to get coffee before heading back home was a stroke of good fortune."

"Sorry you missed me there," Angie said. "I left a bit early."

"Oh, it's fine," Lydia said. "We were in town shopping anyway. I wanted to get some souvenirs to bring home to my friends. Your town is so quaint. I love it."

"It probably isn't like anything you would see down in Florida," Angie said. "Lydia, this is Maggie, by the way. She was at the party, but I don't know if the two of you got a chance to talk much. Mags, this is Lydia, my brother's fiancée."

"It's nice to meet you," Maggie said. "I know I saw you at Angie's house, but I don't think I ever introduced myself."

"Nice to meet you too," Lydia said, shaking her hand. "Have you lived here your whole life?"

"Most of it," Maggie said. "I moved away for a few years, then came back."

"What's it like, spending your life in a tiny town like this? How do you keep from going crazy? How on earth do you stand the cold? I can't even imagine choosing to live here. If I had been born here, I would have moved away as soon as possible." She gave an exaggerated shiver.

Maggie blinked. "Well... it really isn't that bad. I kind of like living in a small town. Everyone knows each other. If I need help with something, I know who to go to. I trust these people. And yeah, it's cold here, but if you dress properly you get used to it pretty quickly. I think it's beautiful here, and I can't see myself ever moving out of Alaska."

"Well, there's all different sorts of people, I suppose,"

Lydia said doubtfully. Angie raised an eyebrow and looked at her brother. She thought Lydia was being a bit rude, but then she didn't know what Jason had told her about his time in Lost Bay.

"You said yourself how gorgeous the scenery is, Lyd," he said, nudging his fiancée with his shoulder. "Not everyone wants to live in a bustling city that never sees snow. Anyway, Angie, I ran into Oliver when we stopped at the diner. We're talking about maybe putting together some flowers and a donation to give to Percy's parents and wife to help cover funeral expenses and whatnot. Are you in?"

"I'll help a bit," she said. "Oliver was still there? He's been there all morning." She told her brother about her short conversation with the other man, and he frowned.

"I'm kind of surprised that he's so upset about Percy's death, to be honest. When Percy was offering me the job, he told me to keep quiet about it because Oliver has been hounding him about it for months. He said Oliver was getting pretty annoyed when he kept getting turned down, and eventually he just stopped talking to Percy altogether. He's not qualified for the position though, so I don't see why he made such a big deal about it."

Angie bit her lip. "That's not quite what he told me. Oliver said that they had been talking a lot recently, and seemed to think that he and Percy were on good terms."

"Odd." Jason rolled his shoulders and drained the last of his coffee. "Well, we're going to take off. I want to drive Lydia down the coast and show her some more of Alaska's natural beauty. We'll make a northerner of her yet."

He waved a quick goodbye to the two of them, then he and Lydia stood up, stuffing her notebook back in her purse, having taken it out to scratch a few items off of another list, and grabbing her coffee. Angie watched them go, her mind stuck on the conversation about Oliver. *I may have been wrong about no one having a reason to want Percy dead*, she thought. *If he found out that Percy offered Jason the job that he wanted, it may have been enough to send him over the edge.*

11

She didn't voice her concerns to Maggie. It was hard to forget how upset her friend had been the night of the party, and she didn't want to bring up bad memories if she could help it. The two of them sat in the coffee house for a while longer, sipping their drinks and talking about in consequential things. After Angie's cup was empty and her head was buzzing with caffeine, she decided that they could probably find a better way to pass the time than just sitting there.

"Any news about your car?" she asked.

"No." Maggie looked sadly at her phone. "They were pretty busy. It will probably be a while yet."

"Is there anything you had to do today? I don't mind driving you."

"Well, I was going to stop at the police station to grab my laptop, which I left there. I want to work on my resume this evening. I'm grateful to my dad for getting me that job, but I don't want to work as a glorified secretary for the rest of my life. I didn't go to college for nothing."

"We can swing by there," she said. "Anything else? Is Josh at a sitter?"

Maggie chuckled as she stood up to throw away her cup. "He's at school, Ange. You know, that place where kids spend a third of their life?"

"Right. I really need to get better at remembering kid stuff if I'm going to get involved with Malcolm." Angie sighed and followed her friend out of the restaurant. "So, the police station. Anywhere else?"

"We could stop at the library, I guess. I've been wanting to pick up a few more books. One nice thing about being divorced is I can stay up as late as I want reading without worrying about my light disturbing anyone. That's about the only nice thing, really. I should have done what you did, and focused on my career instead of getting married right out of college. Not that I regret having Josh — he's my entire reason for living."

"You're still young, you've got plenty of time to find work that you love. What are you thinking of doing?"

They got into the car and Angie started the engine. Maggie waited until they were both buckled in to respond.

"Well, my degree is in psychology. I think I might qualify for a position as a school counselor. I don't know if the local school has any open positions, though. I suppose we could move if I find the right job elsewhere, but Josh has only recently settled in to the school here and I don't want to make him start all over elsewhere. If I have to, I'll just keep working at the police station. At least it's secure and reliable."

"I'm sure your dad likes having you there," Angie said. She guided the car down the street, careful to watch the speed limit. It would be just a bit too ironic if they got pulled over on their way to the police station.

"He's another reason I don't want to move again.

He'd be all alone here if it wasn't for me and Josh, and I know he loves having his grandson around."

Angie didn't doubt that for an instant. She wondered how her parents would feel about having grandchildren. She didn't see wedding bells on her horizon anytime soon, but for all she knew, Jason and Lydia were planning on having kids as soon as they got married. She could be an aunt by this time next year. The thought made her smile.

The police station's parking lot was empty except for two squad cars and a silver sedan. She parked close to the door and shut the engine off, unbuckling herself to go in with her friend. She wished she could ask Maggie how the investigation into Percy's death was going, but she doubted her friend would know anything even if she did want to talk about it. Her father wasn't the sort of person who would share information about an ongoing investigation, not even with his daughter.

There was an older woman inside, behind the front desk. She smiled brightly when she saw Maggie, and Angie stepped forward when her friend introduced her.

"It's nice to meet you, Mrs. Brown," she said, shaking the older woman's hand.

"It's nice to meet you too, dear. Would either of you like anything? Officer Jace's wife brought in cookies this morning, and I think we still have a few left over."

"Thanks, but I'm all right," Maggie said. "I'm just here to grab my computer."

"Your father brought it into the back when he saw you left it here," Mrs. Brown said. "He didn't want to risk it getting stolen, though I don't know who would be silly enough to try to steal something from here."

"I'll go get it from him. Are you okay to wait out here, Angie?"

"Yep. Go ahead, I'm not in a hurry."

Angie turned to the row of chairs against the far wall, but stopped mid-stride when she saw the woman who was already sitting in one of them. It took her a moment to realize why she looked so familiar.

"Esme?" she said. The other woman looked up. Angie had been right; it was Percy's wife.

"Do I know you?" she asked.

"I'm Angie," Angie said, walking over to sit next to her. "The party was at my parents' house."

Esme did not need clarification about which party she was speaking of. "I remember you now. What are you doing here?"

"My friend works here, I'm just waiting for her to pick up something she left." She bit her lip to keep from asking the same question in return. Obviously, Esme was here about her husband's death, but Angie was itching to know the details. It turned out that she didn't have to ask.

"I'm waiting to talk to the detective in charge of my husband's case," she said. "I need to know if he's made any progress."

Angie didn't know what to say to that that wouldn't sound like false comfort or a press for more information. "I hope he has," she said at last. "I'm friends with his daughter so I've known him for a long time. He'll do his best to figure out what happened."

"Thank you," the other woman said. "These past few days feel like a nightmare I can't get myself to wake up from. I'm staying at a hotel because I don't know

Percy's parents that well, and even though we've been married for five years, I'd feel like I was intruding on their grief. I have no one to talk to, and I just feel so guilty because we had an argument the night he left to come visit here. I almost didn't agree to fly up when he asked me to, but I'm so glad I did because I got to have a last few hours with him that I wouldn't have otherwise."

"I'm sorry," Angie said. "I... don't really know what to say because I know that nothing I can say will make you feel better. But what happened to your husband is wrong and I wish I could help you in some way."

"What happened to him?" The other woman focused on her more intently. "That doesn't sound like you think it was an accident."

Angie winced internally. She hadn't meant for it to come out like that. No matter how curious she was about what had happened, the last thing she wanted was to talk to the man's grieving wife about it.

"I didn't mean for it to come out like that."

"Do you know something about what happened to him?" the other woman asked, leaning forward. "Do you know who did it?"

"I have no idea," she said. A moment later, Oliver's face flashed across her mind, but she didn't say anything. She didn't want to set Esme off in the wrong direction, and she was pretty sure falsely accusing someone of murder was a crime. Oliver's behavior might be suspicious, but that didn't mean he was guilty. "I really don't know anything, I just don't understand how he could have fallen off the balcony on his own. The railing is pretty high, that's all."

"I heard him arguing with someone out there," Esme said, lowering her voice. "I told the detective that. I went to go look for him to let him know the food was ready, and I heard him arguing with someone and decided to wait for a while. His business is his business, and with how rocky our relationship has been lately, I didn't think he'd appreciate me intervening."

"Do you know who he was arguing with?"

The other woman shook her head. "His voice was the only one raised. I just *know* whoever it was is the one who killed him. I didn't see him again after that. I probably should have been concerned, but I didn't even realize how long it had been."

"I'm sure Detective O'Brien will figure it out," Angie

said. The door that led to the back opened and she saw Maggie come through. She stood up, relieved to have an excuse to go. She didn't want to say the wrong thing to Esme, and didn't know how to handle this sort of discussion with someone who had been so close to the deceased. "There's my friend, I've got to get going. Good luck. Just hang in there."

She almost gave the other woman a smile, but decided that would be odd given the circumstances, and settled for an awkward half wave as she hurried over to Maggie. She looked over her shoulder as they left the building and saw Esme sitting with her head in her hands. Her heart twisted. *I could have handled that better*, she thought. She knew she should be better at talking to people who had lost a loved one — she had lost someone herself, after all — but somehow no matter how sincere she was, her words ended up sounding fake. The best she could do was hope that Esme would get her closure, and would at some point find peace.

1 2

When Angie got home, her father's truck was still gone which meant that Jason and Lydia were still out. She wanted to talk to her brother, but it would have to wait. After saying a quick hello to her parents, she grabbed a tennis ball from the closet and took Petunia outside with her. The old dog might not have as much energy as she did when she was younger, but she still needed exercise, and the fresh — if cold — air would do Angie good as well.

She spent a while tossing the ball for the husky, who was enthusiastic about chasing it, but not so enthusiastic about bringing it back. After she had had enough of chasing an amused dog through the snow to try to grab the slobbery ball, she decided to change gears and go on a walk. Her parents property was expansive, with groomed trails for the sleds that made it tough to get lost. *It really is beautiful out here*, she thought as she watched Petunia run through the snow ahead of her. She could understand why her parents had never wanted to leave.

On her way back from the walk, she stopped by the dog yard and slipped through the gate to check on Oracle, who seemed happy to be back out in the snow with his teammates. The other dogs yipped and howled for her attention, and she found herself going around to each to greet them and give them belly rubs. Even though nothing had changed, something about being around the dogs made her feel better. Talking to Esme had put her in a melancholy mood, but it was hard to stay sad around such joyful animals.

By the time she made it back to the house, her brother and Lydia were home. She brushed the snow off of Petunia and went inside, immediately finding herself surrounded by warmth and the promising smell of food. She followed the voices into the kitchen, where she found her family sitting around the table, to-go boxes from the diner spread out in front of them.

"Hey, Ange," her brother said. "Grab a seat. None of us felt like cooking, so we decided to pick something up for dinner. We got you a BLT and fries."

"Sounds great," she said, sitting down next to Lydia and grabbing her food.

"It's so nice to have you both here," her mother said. "You need to visit more often, Jason."

"Yeah." Her brother wiped his mouth with a napkin and leaned back in his chair. "About that. You know the job that Percy offered me? Well, assuming nothing changes at the research center once they get reorganized, I might consider applying. If I can convince Lydia to move up here, anyway. We were talking about moving after our wedding — neither of us want to raise our kids in Miami — and this job is something I've always wanted to do. It pays well, too."

"Jason, that would be wonderful," their mother said.

"We'd live in Anchorage, so we wouldn't be super close, but I could visit more often and help Dad out with some of the projects he mentioned he wanted to do. And that way you two could get to know your grandkids, and Angie would be able to be an aunt."

He glanced at his wife. "It's not certain yet, of course. I don't want to get your hopes up. There are other things to consider, even if the job is still available."

Lydia's smile looked like it was frozen on her face. "I'm not sure I'd be happy up here, dear. Your family is lovely, but I like my beaches sunny, not icy. There are perfectly good jobs in Florida for you to take."

"I know." He patted her hand. "We can talk about it later."

The conversation was stilted after that. Lydia didn't have much to say to anyone, and Angie's mother kept glancing hopefully at Jason. Her father finished his burger, then got up to get ice cream out of the fridge. Angie rose when he did and started clearing the table. Just as her father started serving the ice cream, someone's phone started ringing in the other room.

"That's mine," Lydia said, jumping up. "I think I left it in my coat pocket."

She hurried out of the room. A moment later, she let out a shriek that had all of them jumping out of their seats and hurrying toward the front door.

"What happened?" Jason asked his fiancée. She was staring at a piece of paper, her eyes wide.

"L-look," she stammered, holding it out to him. He took it and read it. Angie saw his face go white.

"What is it?" she asked. He handed it over to her silently.

LEAVE OR YOU'RE NEXT was scribbled on it in messy writing. Angie gulped and handed it over to her parents, glancing between her brother and his fiancée in concern.

"You just found that in your pocket?"

Lydia nodded, still looking shaken. "I felt it in there earlier today, but I thought it was just a receipt. I felt it again when I went to grab my phone and took it out, meaning to throw it away. Then I saw what was written on it..." She trailed off. Jason stepped closer to her and pulled her into his arms.

"It's okay," he said. "We'll figure out who left it there."

"Do you think this has something to do with what happened to Percy?" their mother asked.

"I'm sure it does," their father said gruffly. "Did you see something someone wouldn't want you to see?"

Lydia shook her head tearfully. "I don't know why anyone would want me gone. Maybe... maybe they meant the note to apply to Jason more than me. If I leave, he leaves."

"I don't know why anyone would want me gone, either," Jason said, looking puzzled.

"Oliver," Angie said, her eyes widening. When they looked at her questioningly, she clarified. "The way he described his friendship with Percy was different from the way Jason said Percy described it. We all know he really wanted that job. Maybe he thinks if he chases Jason out of town, the job will be his — even though that doesn't really make sense now that Percy is gone. You guys saw him at the diner earlier today, didn't you? He could have slipped the note into Lydia's pocket then."

"If that's true, then he doesn't know what he's dealing with," Jason said, tightening his arms around his fiancée. "I'm not letting anyone scare us away."

13

True to his word, Jason refused to cut his trip short, even though Lydia begged him to find tickets for an earlier flight home. Personally, Angie thought that he should at least send Lydia back to Florida early, even if he didn't want to go. If whoever had left that note was responsible for Percy's death, then there was no telling what they might do when they found out Jason and Lydia hadn't listened. His fiancée would be safer out of state. Though she couldn't blame Lydia for not wanting to leave Jason, especially if his life was in danger as well.

The next few days were fraught with concern for all of them, but when no further threats were made, they began to relax again. On Thursday morning, Angie went into the diner like usual, spending the morning making breakfast for their customers. Betty came in around mid-afternoon, and gave Angie a bright smile when she saw her.

"I bet you were relieved to hear the news," she said.

"What news?" Angie asked, confused. She hadn't had time to do anything more than stumble from her bed to the shower to the car that morning, and had left the radio in the kitchen playing on a music station, so if something new had happened, she was unaware.

"The police ruled that poor young man's death an accident this morning," she said. "It must be such a relief to your family, and to his. It's still heartbreaking, of course, but foul play would be so much harder to deal with."

Angie blinked, not sure what to say or how she should be feeling. She had spent the past few days assuming that Percy had been murdered, which tied in perfectly to the note Lydia had found in her pocket. If what the police had ruled was accurate... then why had someone left her brother and his fiancée a threatening note?

"That's... good," she said. "I had no idea they closed the case already. Thanks for letting me know."

Betty tsked. "You really should start watching the news. It's very enlightening. The local station might not be glamorous, but it's the only way to stay on top of things. You know, I've been telling your father for ages that we should put a television in here. A nice screen, right over the counter in the dining area. We'd get people in to watch sports on the weekends, and we could keep the news on the rest of the time."

"I'll talk to him about it," Angie promised, only half paying attention. "Do you mind if I take a short break? I want to call my brother. Percy was a friend of his, you know."

"Of course, dear. Take as long as you need. It doesn't look like we're very busy at the moment."

She grabbed the diner's landline and sat down at a stool in the nook where the employees kept their things. It wasn't very private, but it was the best she could do. She dialed her parents' phone — her brother's cell phone didn't get great service at the house — and waited for her mother to get Jason on the line. She told him the news.

"They decided that already?" He sounded irritated. "I knew we should have taken the note to them."

Angie sighed. Lydia had been the one to insist that they didn't involve the police with the threat. She didn't want to cause any more trouble than was necessary, and had apparently watched one too many television dramas where calling the police was the wrong thing to do. In Angie's book, calling the police was the *only* thing to do when one received a death threat.

"It's not too late," she said. "You could still bring it to them. I wish we hadn't all handled it so much. They might have been able to get finger prints off of it."

"I'll talk to Lydia," he said. "But if they already closed the case, I'm not sure if it will matter. They'll probably wonder why we didn't give it to them earlier."

Well, they'd be right, she thought, but she didn't say it. Her brother had just reunited himself with the family, and she didn't want to chance driving him away again. "I guess it's up to you. Let me know what they say if you do bring it in."

"I will," he promised.

Angie heard the bell over the diner's door ring. Betty

hurried out of the kitchen to seat whoever had come in. "I should get going," she said. "I'm at work. I'll see you later tonight."

"See you, Ange. Thanks for letting me know about Percy."

They said their goodbyes and she put the phone back in the cradle. Not a second later, Betty came bustling back through the door to the kitchen.

"You've got two people out front wanting to see you," she said. "One of them looks very distraught. Take your time with them. I'll get everyone waters."

Puzzled, Angie thanked her and hurried out into the dining area to find Maggie and Esme sitting side by side at a booth. Esme's face was streaked with tears, and Maggie was trying to comfort her. She looked up when Angie approached, her expression turning relieved.

"Thank goodness. I didn't know where else to bring her."

"What's going on?" Angie asked.

"She came into the police station and started yelling at everyone," Maggie said. "She was so upset when she heard her husband's death was ruled an accident. I left early to bring her here and try to help her calm down."

"Esme?" Angie said softly. "Can I get you anything? Would you like some tea?"

The other woman nodded tearfully. "Tea would be nice. Thank you."

"I'll be right back," Angie promised. "The three of us will talk about this. It will be okay, Esme. You've got two sympathetic ears at your disposal."

Angie returned with three cups of tea and the water that Betty had poured for them. She set the tray down on the table and took a seat across from Esme and Maggie. She was glad that the diner was relatively quiet; it gave them the chance to talk in peace.

"Here you go," she said. "It's chamomile."

It took Esme a few minutes to calm down. She held the mug with tea in it in her hands as if it was keeping her alive, sipping it every few seconds and taking deep, shuddering breaths.

"Sorry," she whispered at last. "I'm so embarrassed.

Thank you so much for getting me out of there before I got myself into trouble, Maggie."

"Don't worry about it. I was happy to help. Do you want to talk about it?"

The other woman shrugged. "I just feel so defeated. Someone killed Percy. I just know it. And now they're going to walk free."

"Maybe not," Angie said. She told the two women about the note Lydia had found. "Whoever did this is still out there, and still making threats."

"I just wish I knew who it was. Who could hate my husband enough to end his life?"

Angie glanced at Maggie and bit her lip. Neither of them knew of her suspicions about Oliver. She knew that it might be smartest to keep her mouth shut, but it didn't feel right keeping this sort of information from the grieving woman.

"There's one person who might have had a motive, and he would have had a chance to slip the note into Lydia's coat pocket too," she admitted. At the other two women's questioning looks, she explained about Oliver. "It all lines up with him. If he heard that Percy was offering Jason the job, he might have been mad enough to confront Percy. If he lost his temper, he could have easily pushed him and caused him to fall. And he was at the diner when my brother and his fiancée stopped in. There would have been plenty of time for him to slip the note into her coat pocket. If he just accidentally killed someone, he might not have been thinking clearly."

"Even if it was an accident, he has to pay for it," Esme said darkly. "I need to know the truth. I want to know why my husband was taken from me before his time."

"I don't know how we could do any snooping ourselves," Angie said hesitantly. "I mean, we can't just go ask Oliver if he killed someone."

"Do you know where he works?"

"He's a teacher at the school. Why?"

"That means we know where he'll be. It would be very easy to find him and ask him just that."

"I don't mean that we physically can't ask him, I mean that it wouldn't be... right." Angie was regretting bringing him up in the first place.

"Well, it's not right that he killed Percy!" Esme's voice

started to rise, and Maggie put a hand on her arm. She glanced at Angie.

"We can at least go talk to him," her friend said. "If he really is guilty, he might not react well to being confronted by Esme. Especially if it was an accident."

She hesitated, but eventually agreed. "All right. But not doing anything that might get us in trouble with the police. I know this is an emotional situation, but getting arrested won't help anything. And we'll have to wait until I'm done with my shift. It's only about another hour, but I can't leave early again. I'll get you guys some food while you wait. Does that work?"

The other two women nodded and Angie got up to get them menus. She had a feeling she was going to regret this, but she had never been great at saying no when someone really needed her help.

14

The two women were still waiting for her when Theo got there and Angie's shift officially ended. She hurried to take off her apron and don her coat. She was sorely regretting agreeing to this — confronting a man at his place of work about a murder was a seriously bad idea, even if they didn't outright accuse him — but she had a feeling that Esme, at least, would go with or without their help. If she and Maggie could play damage control, they might be able to keep the other woman from getting arrested, or hurt.

"We can take my car," she offered. "The school should be getting out in a couple of minutes. Then we can go in and see if we can find Oliver."

They agreed and piled into the van that Angie's

father had given her when she first arrived. The school wasn't far from the center of town, and she ended up driving around the block twice until she saw buses lining up and students flooding the lawn. Lost Bay was small enough to have only one school for all grades, and the crowd of children was a controlled chaos. An old van idling in the parking lot while school was in session probably would have raised some red flags, and she definitely did *not* want to be responsible for the school going into lockdown.

They waited until the buses had gone and most of the students had left before parking and getting out of the van. Maggie led them to the front doors, and all three of them filed inside. The school had been updated somewhat since Angie had gone there, and she spent a moment looking around curiously. It all seemed so much smaller now.

"Where's the computer lab?" she asked Maggie.

"Um, I think it's this way. Josh doesn't have that class, and I've only been here once for parent-teacher conferences. It feels weird being here without him. I feel kind of bad that he's on his way to the sitter's house, while I'm not even working."

They followed her down a hallway, and after a couple of wrong turns, found the computer lab. Angie had been half hoping that Oliver would have left as soon as his class let out, but he was sitting at the desk in the front of the room, working on something on his computer. He looked up when they came in and a puzzled expression crossed his face.

"Can I help you?"

Esme started forward, but Maggie put a hand on her arm and shook her head. Both women turned to look toward Angie, as if expecting her to take the lead. *I didn't even want to come here,* she thought. *Why did I let myself get dragged into this? And how on earth am I supposed to start this conversation?*

"Any luck with the job hunt?" she asked, saying the first thing that popped into her mind. Her voice came out way too cheery, and she winced.

Oliver raised an eyebrow and shook his head. "No. And please keep your voice down. I don't want the principal to hear that I'm looking for another job. He might decide to replace me before I've found one."

"Sorry." She winced. "Um, I take it you've heard the news? The police ruled Percy's death an accident."

"I saw it on the news this morning. I'm glad they solved that."

"They didn't solve anything," Esme said, apparently unable to keep quiet any longer. "I know he didn't just slip and fall off that balcony. Someone pushed him."

Oliver stared at her, as if unsure what to say.

"This was a bad idea," Maggie said quietly.

"No it wasn't," Esme snapped. She turned back to Oliver. "I know you killed him. Angie told me all about how upset you were that he wouldn't give you a job you were unqualified for, and how you slipped that death threat into her brother's fiancée's pocket. It's just pure luck on your part that they didn't decide to take that note to the police. I'm sure they would have been able to analyze your handwriting and have you in cuffs in a heartbeat."

"I have absolutely no idea what you're talking about," Oliver said. He sounded more annoyed than anything, and Angie began to doubt her suspicions. Surely if he was guilty, he would have more of a reaction to being accused outright like that?

"Maybe he's telling the truth," Maggie said. "Esme,

take a deep breath. Can you think of any way to prove that Oliver is responsible for any of this?"

The other woman fell silent for a moment. "He's the only one," she said at last, her voice hoarse. "You said it yourself, he's the only one who makes everything fit."

"I don't know what's going on, but none of you should really be here," Oliver said. He shut off his monitor and stood up. "Only one of you even has a student in this school. I could get all three of you removed by the police for trespassing, but I'd really rather not have to go that far. Please leave."

"I'm not leaving until you admit to killing my husband."

Oliver's expression darkened. "If anyone killed him," he said, "it's you."

15

The accusation seemed to hit Esme like a punch to the gut. "You... I didn't... He was my husband!"

"We talked about other things than just the open job position," Oliver said. "He told me all about your rocky relationship. He even said that you brought up separation a couple of times. Isn't the spouse always the first suspect in these things?"

"Our relationship wasn't perfect, but that doesn't mean I didn't love him," Esme said. She sounded like she was nearing tears again. "You have no right to accuse me of something like that."

"You don't have any right to come in here and accuse me of it either," he said. He began shoving papers into a messenger bag. "Maybe I should call the police. I bet they don't know half of the issues the two of you had. I'm sure they would have dug a lot deeper into his case if they knew how tough of a time you two were having. I guess they figured you might not have much of a motive, since he didn't have a life insurance policy. A divorce would be better for you financially than killing him would be."

"He had a life insurance policy," Esme said. "You're just making things up."

"He stopped paying on it," Oliver said. He sounded like he was forcing his voice to remain casual. "He told me in an email after I asked about the benefits that the job offered. He said there was a life insurance policy, but it didn't cover any work-related accidents, and it wasn't worth the money. He canceled it. I can show you the email, if you'd like."

Esme stared at him for a long moment. Angie watched her, half wondering if she really had killed her husband, expecting to get a large payoff once he was gone. But the other woman's face had a look of stricken sadness on it. *If she killed him, then she's the best actor I've ever seen*, Angie thought, remembering the tears Esme had shed at the diner.

Oliver's words seemed to have deflated something

inside of her. "He... didn't tell me," she whispered. "He didn't share that with me. What else didn't he share? I wasted so much time being petty with him. I should have done better."

Oliver sighed. "Look, I didn't kill your husband. I'm sorry he's dead, and I wish you the best. But I'm going to ask you one last time to please leave. This is a school, and it isn't appropriate for you to come here and make these accusations. If you want to contact the police and see if you can convince them to question me again, go ahead. I'll happily let them read our correspondence. I have nothing to hide, unless you count hiding the fact that I'm looking for a new job from the principal."

"Come on," Maggie said. "We should go, Esme." The other woman nodded and let herself be guided out of the room.

"I'm sorry," Angie told Oliver, then followed them.

It was a quiet group that walked back out to the van. The three of them climbed in and put on their seat belts. Angie started the engine, but didn't pull out of the parking lot. She wasn't sure where to go.

"I guess maybe the police were right," Esme said

softly. "Maybe it was an accident, and I'm just grasping at straws."

Angie was about to agree with her when she remembered the note. She shook her head.

"No. Lydia wouldn't have gotten a death threat if it was nothing. We're missing something."

"Angie," Maggie said, her voice urgent. "Lydia."

Angie turned to look at her friend. "What?"

"All of the pieces fit with her too. Think about it. She could have written the note herself, to convince Jason to go back home. You heard her at the coffee shop. She hates this place. She didn't say so outright, but it's obvious she wouldn't be able to stand living here."

"So she wrote herself a death threat? I could maybe see that, I guess. That would mean that Percy's death really was an accident, and she basically sent us all off on a wild goose chase."

Maggie shook her head. "No. What if she killed him?"

Angie stared at her friend, her eyes widening. "But she doesn't have a motive."

"Was she there when Percy offered Jason the job?"

Slowly, Angie nodded. "Yeah. They were both talking to me when he dragged them away."

"If he acted really excited about it and started talking about moving here... well, it's a stretch, but maybe she went back to try to talk Percy out of offering the job, and when he wouldn't capitulate, she lost her temper."

She bit her lip and glanced in the back, where Esme was staring at her intently.

"I... I don't know. I'll poke around when I get home, okay?"

Maggie nodded. After a moment's hesitation, Esme also nodded.

"Promise me that you'll try to find out the truth."

"I promise."

16

Angie dropped Esme and Maggie off at the diner, where Maggie's car was, then drove home. Her mind wandered during the drive as she thought about everything her friend had said. She had never even considered Lydia as a suspect. She had convinced herself that the other woman was practically family, but really, how well did they know her? Jason was the only one who had known her for more than a few days, and she knew her brother always tended to only see the best in people. There was no way he would ever even pause to wonder if someone he loved had committed a crime.

The note, she decided, was the biggest piece of evidence that they had. If there was some way she could match the handwriting on the note to Lydia's handwriting... but no, she remembered the scribbled words. There was no way Lydia wouldn't have tried to disguise her writing if she had written the note herself.

She parked in front of the house and let herself inside, greeting Petunia and taking off her outerwear before going into the kitchen to get a drink. Lydia and Jason were both in there, playing a board game on the kitchen table. Angie froze, staring at Lydia, her mind still trying to work out the problem of how to prove her guilt — or her innocence.

"Hey, Ange," Jason said. "Pull up a chair. You can join us for the next round."

"Thanks, but I'm going to take a break for a while. I've been around people all day." She gave her brother a weak smile and poured herself a glass of milk before stepping out of the room. She paused on her way by the living room. Lydia's purse was sitting on the coffee table, unattended. She remembered the little notebook she had seen the other woman write in on and off during her stay and had an idea.

"Hey, Lydia?" she said, walking back to the kitchen. "Do you have that note?"

"Your dad put it on the fridge," Lydia said. "Why?"

"My friend Maggie wanted to see it. Do you mind if I send her a picture?"

She thought Lydia hesitated for a fraction of a second before agreeing. Her heart pounding, Angie walked over to the fridge and removed the note that her father had pinned up under a magnet, as if it was a child's drawing and not a death threat.

"Thanks," she called as she left the room again, note in one hand and a glass of milk in the other. She stepped into the living room and carefully opened Lydia's purse, feeling as though she might jump out of her skin at any second. She grabbed the notebook and hurried to her bedroom, Petunia on her heels.

"You might as well come in," she said, holding the door open for the dog. Once Petunia was in the room, Angie shut and locked the door, put her glass of milk on her nightstand, and sat down on the bed. The note had been written on lined paper that had been torn jaggedly from its source. As soon as she opened the notebook, she had the feeling she was on the right track. The paper was identical to what the notebook had inside of it. Still, she flipped through the little notebook until she came to a page that had been torn out. She held the note up to the torn page and felt the breath whoosh out of her. It was a match. She stared at the notebook and the page for a second, then stood up. Anger was beginning to make her palms prickle. *This might not be evidence that Lydia killed someone, but it* is *evidence that she made up a death threat just because she wanted to go home sooner.*

Her hands shaking, she left her bedroom and strode back toward the kitchen. Not pausing for an instant, not even to think, she dropped the paper and the notebook in front of Jason.

"She wrote it," she spit out, glancing at Lydia. "She lied to all of us."

She saw the gears turning in Jason's head as he looked between the note and the ripped page it had obviously come from. Lydia made a grab for the paper, but he yanked it away in time.

"Is this true?" he asked his fiancée.

"Jason, sweetie —"

"Is it?"

Her lower lip quivered. "I just wanted to get out of

this horrible cold and go home. I miss my beaches and good food. Remember our favorite pizza place? Those slices we got here don't even start to compare."

"So you faked a death threat?" Jason asked, his voice deadly calm as he stared at her.

She bit her lower lip. "Can't you forgive me?"

Her brother opened his mouth to respond, but Angie cut in. "Did you kill him?" she asked, her voice just above a whisper.

"Of course not. Don't be silly," she said, glancing toward the floor.

The breath whooshed out of Jason. "You're lying."

"You don't have any right to accuse me of —"

"Stop," he said, holding up a hand. Angie's heart broke at the expression on his face. "I know you well enough to tell when you're lying. What happened, Lydia? And think before you start talking. If you lie to me about this, I will drive you personally to the police station and after I drop you off you will never see me again."

"I... I... It was an accident." Lydia's voice broke and she buried her face in her arms. Her voice came out muffled. "After I dragged you away from him, I marched back out to the balcony and told him to withdraw the job offer, because there was no way we were moving here. He told me you had a right to decide for yourself and then he grabbed my shoulder and tried to guide me back inside, but I was mad that he thought he could shove me around, so I pushed him. I wasn't even thinking, I swear I didn't mean for him to fall. It all happened so fast. He went over the edge of the balcony and I heard a crack when he landed and I looked over the railing and he wasn't moving and... and..." She took a deep breath and raised her head. "And I went back inside and pretended nothing happened even though I was falling apart inside."

The kitchen fell silent after that. Angie put her hand on her brother's shoulder. He didn't seem to know what to say, and she didn't blame him. There were no words for something like this. Lydia started crying again and Petunia walked over to her. The dog nudged her hand with her muzzle, not under-standing what was happening.

Angie heard her father's heavy tread as he approached the kitchen. He paused in the doorway, taking in the scene in front of him.

"What's going on?"

EPILOGUE

Angie gripped her mother's arm tightly as they watched Jason walk through security at the airport. He turned to wave at them, and all three of them waved back. A moment later, he was gone, lost in the crowd that was headed for the gates. Angie's father let out a slow sigh.

"That was some visit."

Angie gave him a weak smile. "Well, on the bright side he's talking to you two again after ten years."

"We'll be lucky if he ever visits again, after what happened here," he grumbled.

Privately, Angie disagreed. She had her doubts that Jason would want to stay in Florida. He had broken things off with Lydia while she was still in the holding cell at the police station. According to him, it had been a long, emotional conversation, one which they were only allowed because Maggie had stepped in and convinced her father to let them meet. With nothing holding him to the sunshine state, she thought he would probably take the job in Anchorage if it was still available after everything settled down.

"Let's head home," Angie's mother said. "I'm exhausted. These past two weeks took a lot out of me."

They walked through the airport in silence. In the parking lot, Angie squeezed into the back seat in the cab of the truck, while her father and mother sat in the front. After they hit the highway outside of town, Angie spoke up again.

"Did you and Jason ever get a chance to talk, Dad?"

He met her eyes in the rearview mirror, and she wondered if he knew what she was talking about. Jason probably hadn't told him that he told her about what their father said after Katy's funeral.

"We did," he said. "We both had some stuff to apologize for. It's all cleared up now."

She nodded, satisfied with that answer. She was still reeling emotionally from the visit, and imagined that everyone involved was feeling the same way. It would be nice for things to get back to normal for a while. With luck, Jason would continue nourishing the renewed relationship he had with their family, and if he took the job in Anchorage, they might be able to start having something like regular visits. Even after Percy's death and Lydia's mess of lies, Angie felt as if their family had managed to heal most of its wounds. She was glad. It was never more important to have people you could rely on than when times were tough, and Jason was probably going through the toughest time imaginable right now.

She leaned her forehead against the window and gazed out at the passing terrain, glad to be going home.

Darling Deli Series

Book 1: Pastrami Murder

Book 2: Corned Beef Murder

Book 3: Cold Cut Murder

Book 4: Grilled Cheese Murder

Book 5: Chicken Pesto Murder

Book 6: Thai Coconut Murder

Book 7: Tomato Basil Murder

Book 8: Salami Murder

Book 9: Hearty Homestyle Murder

Book 10: Honey BBQ Murder

Book 11: Beef Brisket Murder

Book 12: Garden Vegetable Murder

Book 13: Spicy Lasagna Murder

Book 14: Curried Lobster Murder

Book 15: Creamy Casserole Murder

Book 16: Grilled Rye Murder

Book 17: A Quiche to Die For

Book 18: A Side of Murder

Book 19: Wrapped in Murder

AUTHOR'S NOTE

I'd love to hear your thoughts on my books, the storylines, and anything else that you'd like to comment on—reader feedback is very important to me. My contact information, along with some other helpful links, is listed below. If you'd like to be on my list of "folks to contact" with updates, release and sales notifications, etc.... just shoot me an email and let me know. Thanks for reading!

Also...

... if you're looking for more great reads, I am proud to announce that Summer Prescott Books publishes several popular series by Cozy authors Gretchen Allen and Patti Benning, as well as Carolyn Q. Hunter, Blair Merrin, Susie Gayle and more!

CONTACT SUMMER PRESCOTT
BOOKS PUBLISHING

Twitter: @summerprescott1

Blog and Book Catalog:
http://summerprescottbooks.com

Email: summer.prescott.cozies@gmail.com

And...look up The Summer Prescott Fan Page and Summer Prescott Publishing Page on Facebook – let's be friends!

To download a free book, and sign up for our fun and exciting newsletter, which will give you opportunities to win prizes and swag, enter contests, and be the first to know about New Releases, click here: http://summerprescottbooks.com

Made in the USA
Lexington, KY
12 June 2019